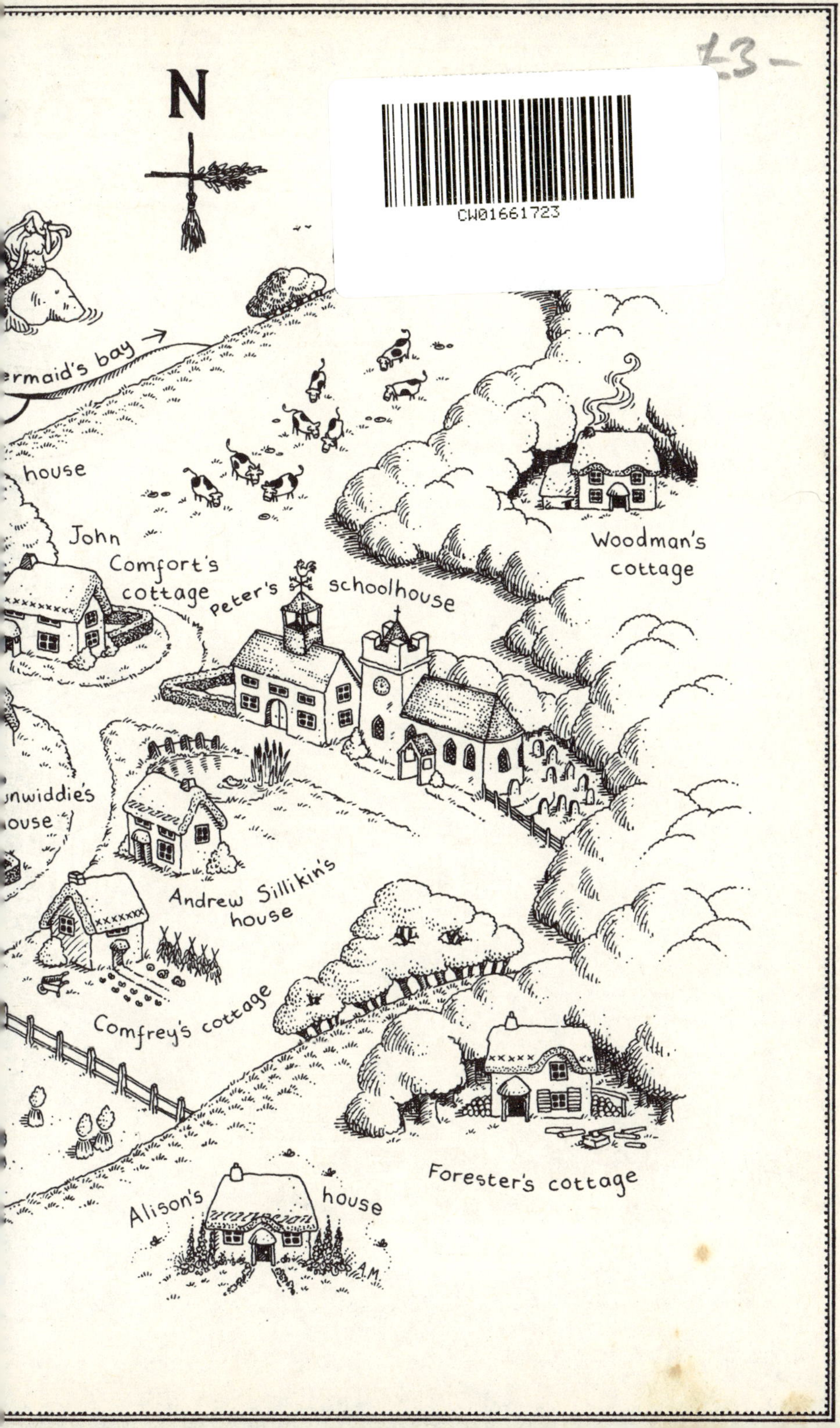
N
ermaid's bay
house
John Comfort's cottage
Peter's schoolhouse
Woodman's cottage
nwiddie's
ouse
Andrew Sillikin's house
Comfrey's cottage
Forester's cottage
Alison's house
A.M.

Magic
from the
Ground

First published in 1990

Printed in England
for J. M. Dent & Sons Ltd
91 Clapham High Street
London SW4 7TA

British Library Cataloguing in Publication Data
Greaves, Margaret
Magic from the ground.
I. Title II. McAllister, Angela
823'.914 [J]

ISBN 0-460-88013-6

MARGARET GREAVES

Magic from the Ground

Illustrated by
ANGELA McALLISTER

J. M. DENT & SONS LTD
LONDON

To my sister, Mary,
who is a mistress of bees.
M. G.

For Sue, with love.
A. McA.

Contents

Read this first!

If you read these stories you may learn a lot about the ancient magic of plants. Very few of us still make use of it. Times have changed. Nowadays we use fertilisers and modern medicine – and they are probably much safer than spells! But your great-great-great-grandparents believed that plants had very strange powers for good or ill. They were right about some things. Modern doctors still use digitalis which comes from foxgloves and belladonna which comes from deadly nightshade. Perhaps our ever-so-great-grandparents had real knowledge about things we have almost forgotten. (Some beekeepers still put juniper near their hives.) Whether they were right or wrong, there is certainly more to plants than most of us know. But don't try to use any of the spells or potions in these stories, although the plants are still to be found in many places if you know where to look. You need the ancient power as well as the herbs and charms, and that power was lost long ago.

The Green Child

There was a poor man called Comfrey who lived in the smallest cottage in Peckington Parva. His bit of garden was no wider than two bean-poles laid end to end, and not a thing would grow in it but goose-grass and nettles. Comfrey had nettle soup for his supper every night, and very tired he was of it.

One evening in late March, while he was making his soup, Comfrey heard an odd noise. He went to the door and listened. Yes, there it was again. Someone was crying in the cold spring twilight. He hurried out into the garden. The light was fading fast, and at first he could seen no one there at all. But still someone sobbed in the garden, and at last he found him. A tiny boy, naked as a fish, was curled up among the nettles, crying his heart out.

'Hey! Hey!' said Comfrey. 'What's all this? Where be you from, little fellow?'

The child looked up at him but said nothing at all. His skin and hair were green as the grass, and the tears in his eyes glittered like emeralds.

If ever a man was frightened, it was Comfrey. He

knew well enough what he had found. It was a fairy's child, lost and crying. Comfrey wanted no doings with the Little People. But, fairy or not, the creature was very young and very unhappy. He couldn't leave him to cry all alone among the nettles.

He picked him up – light as a leaf he was and cold as a frog – and carried him indoors. The child stopped crying, but said never a word all evening. Comfrey fed him with nettle soup and brown bread, wrapped him in his own blanket, and nursed him until he slept.

All that week the fairy boy stayed in the cottage. Comfrey fed him and warmed him, and even made him a little suit of clothes out of his only spare pair of breeches. The child watched him with his strange green eyes, but was always silent. Sometimes he cried quietly to himself.

Late on the Saturday night Comfrey heard a shrill voice calling from the garden.

'My son! Are you there? My son, my son!'

The child jumped up laughing and ran to the door.

'Open it! Open it! Quickly!'

Comfrey opened the door and the little creature darted out without a goodbye or a backward look.

'Here I am,' he cried. 'Here I am.'

Comfrey stood in the doorway, too frightened to cry out. The shrill voice called again out of the darkness.

'Comfrey! A blessing on your garden, for you've been kind to my boy. Dig up the nettles and grow what you will.'

Next day Comfrey dug up all the nettles, and in their place set the seeds of cabbages and beans and carrots and potatoes. He watered them and watched them and waited, and in time the carrots and potatoes showed their first specks of green. But there was never a sign of the cabbages and beans. The soil looked grey and dead and cold, and the nettles began to grow there again, thicker than ever.

'I'll soon be as badly off as I was before,' thought poor Comfrey. 'They nettles will spoil everything else that's agrowing. I think the little lad's father meant kindly by me. Maybe he won't mind if I ask for help. Yet they be unchancy creatures. Suppose it makes 'un angry?'

He thought anxiously, for the Little People can be dangerous. But in the end he gave his last coin to a wise woman for a pot of the ointment that gives sight of the fairies. She had made it of the buds of hollyhocks, marigolds, wild thyme, and the buds of young hazels. These she had mixed with grass from an ant-hill, which country people call a fairy throne, covered it all with oil and left it in the sun for three days.

'Have a care how you use it,' she warned him. 'They're secret folk and don't like to be disturbed.'

Comfrey's heart was beating very fast when at twilight, the fairy time, he climbed up the hill behind his cottage. Beneath a hawthorn tree, which is a favourite of the Little People, he rubbed his eyes with the ointment. Then he spoke as loudly as he dared.

'Here I be,
Under the hawthorn tree.
Come out from the hill and let me see.'

'Why do you disturb us, Comfrey?' asked a thin cold voice. 'Did I not give you a blessing?'

Comfrey opened his eyes. Near him stood a small man all in green, with thistledown hair that blew in the wind. His eyes were sharp as needles.

'Well,' thought Comfrey to himself, 'I've done it now. 'Tis danger whether I ask or not, so I may as well ask.'

He spoke out boldly, but as politely as he could.

'You did give me a blessing, sir, and grateful I be. But summat goes wrong. The carrots and the taties grows finely, but there's never a sign of the cabbages and beans, and that part of the garden's near ruined again.'

'When did you sow them?' asked the fairy.

'I sowed 'un all one evening,' said Comfrey. 'Six weeks ago come Monday.'

The fairy crowed with laughter, shrill and thin, like the crackle of breaking ice.

'You great fool, you!' said he. 'Six weeks ago come Monday was the dark of the moon – the time to sow plants that grow down into the dark of the earth. But cabbages and peas come up into the light. You must sow *them* when the moon is rising.'

His laughter whistled away on the wind, and Comfrey was left all alone on the hill in the oncoming dark.

Back he hurried, cleared away the nettles, and waited for the first night of a rising moon. Then under its cold grey light he sowed his cabbages and beans for the second time.

The moon waxed and the moon waned. Then with her next rising up came the little green shoots from his seeds, perky and bright as spring rain.

After that Comfrey always remembered to sow his roots in the dark of the moon, and his green plants at her rising. His crops were the best in the village and he never had to eat nettle soup again.

The Apple Tree Man

Apple trees are special trees, touched with magic. Years ago and years ago everyone knew that. Their owners tended them and talked to them, they asked them to bear fruit and they thanked them for the apple harvest. In every orchard the biggest and oldest tree was the king of it, and he was called the Apple Tree Man. The children of Peckington Parva often asked for the old story of the Apple Tree Man and the two sons of a rich farmer.

The farmer lived in a big comfortable farmhouse. He had cornfields and pasture, and one old apple orchard with a tumbledown cottage at one corner of it. He taught his sons what to do to make sure of a good apple crop, and Giles listened because he loved the trees. His younger brother, Jack, said they were daft not to cut them down and sell them for firewood. The trees were too old to be any good.

He was a sharp clever boy, was Jack. He looked at every penny and would never waste even a handful of straw. But Giles would rather give a thing than sell it. Even so, the younger son was the father's favourite, and when he died he left all he had to Jack – 'though I know,' he said, 'that you'll do right by your brother Giles.'

He might have known better, for Jack was spoiled and selfish and cocky, and he'd married a clever greedy wife.

'You can't help your brother,' she said. 'He's a fool, a good-for-nothing dreamer.'

'You're right,' agreed Jack. 'He'd only waste anything I give him.'

But his conscience nagged him a little until he hit on a good idea.

'Brother,' he said, 'I'd like to give you something our father valued. You shall have the little cottage in the apple orchard. And that old ox and the donkey that he's had so many years.'

Both the animals were too old to do much work, and since his father's death Jack had neglected them. They were weak and thin and miserable. But Giles took them gladly. He cut great heaps of grass for them from the roadside. He rubbed their sores with healing herbs – garlic and the flowers of red thistle, and valerian that is still called 'all-heal' to this very day. He loved them and talked to them and let them out in the old orchard until they grew well and strong. He worked hard to repair the cottage, and he pruned the trees and remembered what his father had taught him. On Twelfth Night he sprinkled them all with warm cider, especially the old Apple Tree Man who was king of the orchard, and he said aloud the ancient wassail rhyme.

Apples and pears with right good corn,
Come in plenty to everyone.
Barnfulls, bagfulls, hatfulls,
And the little heap under the stairs.

On St Swithin's Day, July 15th, he sprinkled all the trees with water so that the saint should send them rain. So with the pruning and the caring and the Twelfth Night wassailing and the apple sprinkling on St Swithin's Day, the trees grew and flourished and gave him a good harvest.

When Jack and his wife saw that the ox and donkey could still work and that the orchard was so fruitful, they grew jealous, and Jack demanded some payment for the animals and the land. but Giles didn't resent it. He was happy in his way of life. Sometimes he would go out at night when the moon turned the grey branches to silver. He would talk to the trees, and especially to the Apple Tree Man. As the wind sighed through them it sometimes seemed as if they talked too in their own language.

It was near Christmas again when Jack heard tell that a treasure had once been hidden somewhere on the farm. He thought the old donkey might know where it was, for he'd worked there so many years. Everyone knows that on Christmas Eve the beasts can talk at midnight, and he determined that he would creep secretly down to the stable that Giles had made and would listen to what they said.

Just as night fell on Christmas Eve, Giles gave an extra feed of hay to his animals and wished them

a happy Christmas. Then, as his father had taught him, he warmed a mug of cider by a fire made of ash wood, and took it out to the orchard with a honey cake dipped in the cider. He sprinkled all the trees and put the honey cake on a forked twig of the Apple Tree Man. The night was quiet and full of stars, and as a soft wind stirred the branches it seemed to him that the tree was whispering.

'Giles,' it said, 'fetch your spade and dig under my roots. There's a great heap of gold down there.'

Never was a man so surprised! None the less, he fetched his spade and dug very carefully so as not to hurt a single root. In a very few minutes he turned up something that glinted in the moonlight, and there indeed was a heap of purest gold.

'It belongs to you and no one else,' whispered the Apple Tree Man, 'for you will use it well and kindly. Take it home and say nothing to your brother.'

Giles carried the treasure to his cottage, quite dazed by his good fortune.

Not long after, Jack came creeping into the orchard. As the church clock struck midnight he opened the stable door a crack, and sure enough the animals were talking to each other.

'There's that greedy young brother of our master's at the door,' said the ox.

'Come to hear about his precious treasure,' said the old donkey.

'He's got no manners to spy on us,' snuffled the ox. 'Do you know where the gold is?'

'I know,' said the donkey with a great bray of laughter. 'But it's certain sure *he'll* never find it, for a better man than he has taken it already.'

At that very minute all the trees in the orchard rustled as if they were laughing too.

Neighbours

When your next-door neighbour is a witch it's as well to be careful.

Old Margery wasn't absolutely a black witch. She'd learned some of the craft from her great-aunt, but there was no real malice in her. But she was old and easily cross, and queer things sometimes happened to those who offended her.

John Comfort, her neighbour, got on with her well enough. He minded his manners and spoke to her kindly. He was a good gardener and sometimes gave her vegetables or a basket of fruit. In return she cured John's youngest child of whooping cough, with the leaves of a little herb-twopence boiled in wine with a spoonful of honey. Margery was specially fond of a fresh crisp lettuce, and John always remembered to give her one of his best.

One day there was only one lettuce left in the row. Those in the next sowing were still too small to pull. Old Margery looked over her hedge and saw the crown of bright green leaves with a heart as crunchy as a nut.

'Neighbour Comfort,' she called. 'That's a fine lettuce that you've got there. I could fancy one like that for my supper.'

'Oh dear!' said John, embarrassed. 'On any other day, dame, you should have it and welcome. But it's the last one left until the others grow and I've promised it to my wife.'

'Oh, you did, did you?' said the old woman.

Her eyes glinted at him, bright and sharp, and she went into her house without another word. John felt a little uneasy, but he wouldn't break a promise to his wife.

Early next morning, with the dew still grey and soft on the grass, he went out as usual to look at his garden. What a sad sight met his eyes! Two-thirds of the young lettuce plants that had been so promising were nibbled almost to the ground. Radishes were uprooted, their red skins scored by little white tooth-marks. Some of the young pea-pods hung empty and ragged on their stalks.

'Oh *no*!' groaned John. 'There's a rabbit got in somehow! Thieving, spoiling little varmint. I'd just like to catch him at it, that's all!'

But catching the rabbit wasn't easy. John watched late at night and early in the morning, but never a glimpse of it could he get. He tidied up the mess, sowed another row of lettuce, and gave old Margery one of the few good ones that were left.

'It's to make up for the one my wife wanted,' he explained.

'That's kind of you, neighbour,' said Margery.

'I see you've had a bit of trouble with your garden.'

'That I have,' agreed John Comfort. 'Some plaguey little rabbit got into it last week.'

'Seems so,' said the old woman. 'Seems so.' She looked at him smilingly, with eyes as blue as periwinkles. 'And rabbits are hard to catch, that's for sure.'

A few days later, when the lettuces were growing nicely, the rabbit got into the garden again. When John saw the damaged plants he swore that this time he would catch it. All that night he sat up and watched. At last, in the cool light just before sunrise, he saw something move among the leaves. He sprang forward to strike at it with his spade, but the creature was off in a flash. As it reached the hedge between the two gardens it turned its head for a second and he saw its eyes. A rabbit's eyes are brown, but these were blue, as blue as periwinkles.

John's heart turned cold. All his half-suspicions about his neighbour were proved true. He stared, shivering, at the place where the rabbit had been. Now he knew what was causing all the trouble. He had to stop it, but he didn't want to meddle with a witch. He worried and worried, until at last he hit on a plan.

A witch can change her shape, but she can't return to her own form again unless she drinks the right potion – a drink made of aniseed and boiled laurel leaves. John realised that somewhere in old Margery's house the potion must be waiting. In a corner of her garden was a great tree that at night-time cast a shadow as black and deep as velvet. Here, greatly daring, John slipped in after dark and hid himself.

He waited a long time. At last the witch's door opened and he saw her in the light from the kitchen as she bent and put something down on the ground outside. He heard the clink of a saucer. A minute or two later a small furry thing went hopping down the path and into his own garden.

When he was sure that it had gone, John crept quietly to the door. There was some liquid in the saucer that smelled like aniseed. He tipped it out, then tried the door. It was unlocked and he went very cautiously inside. On the table stood a bowl of murky greenish water, and beside it a small jar filled with seeds. He put the jar in his pocket, then went out again to wait in the shadow of the tree.

Just before dawn a little brown rabbit came hopping up the path to the witch's door. It put its nose to the empty saucer, then gave a thin squeal of alarm. John reached it in three strides while it still searched for any trace of the vanished potion. He picked it up by the scruff of its neck.

'Dame Margery,' he said reproachfully, 'this is a sad state of affairs. Haven't we always been good neighbours? But now you've spoiled my garden and I've stolen your shape-changing charm.'

The rabbit kicked furiously with its feet, but John held it fast.

'I daren't put you down,' he said, 'for there's that great black tom-cat comes hunting round here every night.'

Again the rabbit gave a little shriek, and he cupped it gently in his big hands, stroking its fur.

'There, don't take on so. I'd not let anything hurt you. Let's make a bargain with each other. You leave my garden be, and I'll help you to make another potion – for you can't do it yourself with those little paws.'

The rabbit's blue eyes flashed at him, and then it began to quiver in his hands. John felt nervous, but it was too late to stop now.

'Give me a sign if it's a bargain,' he said.

The rabbit flattened its ears and nibbled quite gently at his finger, so he took it as a sign. He carried it in and set it on the kitchen table, and filled a saucer with the murky green liquid. Then he took from his pocket the little bottle of aniseed.

'How many of these?' he asked.

Nine times the rabbit lifted its paw and nine seeds he dropped into the saucer. As the little creature scurried to drink he saw that it was shaking, and he feared that old Margery must be in a terrible rage. She swallowed thirstily till all the potion was gone.

John held his breath and watched. The house was so still he could have heard even the flutter of a moth's wing. Then suddenly the rabbit disappeared, and standing by the table was old Margery. She was shaking with laughter.

'Fair enough, John Comfort, fair enough,' she said. 'You'd wit enough to find me out, and courage enough to catch me. I'll do no harm to you or yours, for you did none to me when you had the chance.

Good luck go with you, neighbour!'

'And good luck to you, dame!' said John.

From that day on there were no better neighbours in the whole of Peckington Parva.

The Master of Bees

Zachary loved his bees. He erected a stone shelter, which beekeepers call a bole, to protect his three straw skeps from the weather. He built it beneath tall trees to shade it from the midday sun. Beside it he made a shallow pond with big smooth stones at the edge so that the bees could sip the water and yet keep their wings dry. He told them all the news of the village, the weddings and funerals, the new babies, the comings and goings of visitors. Bees, in their strange and secret lives, like to know these things and will leave if their owner fails to talk to them. Being so well cared for, they yielded a wonderful honey harvest every year.

One hot morning in mid-May the first swarm of the year took off from Zachary's best hive. He followed its flight at once, for a swarm can be lost if the beekeeper loses sight of it. He had to watch where it settled and then gently shake the bees into an empty skep. But he was horrified to see the small black cloud soar upwards and then drop straight into Mrs Dunwiddie's chimney. Mrs Dunwiddie was a rich old widow with a very bad temper, but she was one of his best customers. A moment later, wildly beating her arms about her head, she ran out shrieking into the village street.

'Help ! Help ! The house if full of bees ! Oh Zachary ! Zachary ! There you are, you wicked old man ! How dare you send your bees down my chimney'

'I'm sorry, Mrs Dunwiddie,' said Zachary unhappily, 'but I didn't send 'em. It's a swarm, that's what it is. There's no one can stop a swarm. There now, you bide out here while I takes 'em. They'll settle quiet as quiet and do you no harm.'

With a little patience he eventually captured his swarm and took it home. But Mrs Dunwiddie swore she would never buy a single jar of his honey ever again. It was a very bad day.

'Drat the bees !' grumbled Zachary. 'My very best customer lost. 'Tis terrible, so it is.'

Two weeks later another swarm took off from another of his hives. Zachary followed it all through the village, across two fields and up a steep hill. He was very hot and tired when to his dismay the bees flew straight to the edge of the wood that crowned the hill, swept upwards and away over the trees. He could follow them no further. Weary and disappointed he trudged home with his empty skep.

'Drat and drat the bees !' he groaned. 'The whole swarm lost. 'Tis terrible, so it is. Terrible !'.

Two troubles often bring a third. So Zachary wasn't really surprised, one morning in late summer, to find one skep broken in pieces on the ground, streaked in places with dark sticky honey, and a few injured bees crawling among the shattered bits. During the night a bear had come down from the forest and eaten all the honey and all the bees in the skep. Zachary gazed at the ruins in horror.

'Drat and drat and *drat* that bear!' he lamented. 'The whole hive lost! 'Tis terrible, so it is! Terrible, terrible!'

Sadly he began to clear up the mess.

'Troubles-z-z, I z-z-ee. Trouble-z-z,' said a deep, sleepy sort of voice.

Zachary turned round. An odd-looking stranger was watching him from the shadow of the hedge, a smallish man in a fuzzy old jacket striped in black and yellow. He had big dark shiny eyes that made Zachary think of the sun on wet blackberries, a very long nose, and a very small chin.

'Trouble enough,' said Zachary bitterly. 'I've never know'd such a summer. My best customer lost, a good swarm gone, and now look what that dratted bear's done! And rain and cold winds all this past month. There'll be the poorest honey flow for years.'

'Dear-r-r, dear-r-r-r! That's bad, that is. Yet thee's treated 'em proper, I z-z-zee. Sha-a-ade and shelter and water. Do 'ee talk to 'em proper?'

'O' course I talk to 'em,' said Zachary. 'Every evening I tells what's happened in the day.'

'That's-s-s r-r-right.' The stranger hummed to himself, scratching his ear with a long thin finger

while he thought. 'Then it must be the juniper,' he said at last.

'Juniper? There be no juniper here.'

'That's it,' murmured the visitor. 'That's-s-s just it. No juniper. Bees-z-z need juniper. Thee get a bit o' juniper, a good big bit. Hang it in the bole there.'

Zachary turned to look where the stranger had pointed. When he looked back there was no one at all in the garden except himself. There was only the drowsy murmur of a voice that faded on the summer air. The bees in the two undamaged skeps hummed to themselves in deep content.

'That was a queer do if ever there was one!' said Zachary.

All the same, he went into the village to a friend of his and begged a branch from his juniper tree. He hung it carefully in the bee bole behind the hives.

All that autumn the bees seemed settled and quiet. He watched them flying in and out and listened to the peaceful hum within the hives. As winter frosted all the garden he still came out every evening to tell them the day's news, and could hear the soft stir of the bees endlessly moving as they pressed round their queen to keep her warm.

Spring broke the frost and softened the earth until on warm days the bees began to fly again. April smothered every orchard with pink apple blossom, and the bees foraged all day long until they could hardly carry the weight of dark pollen in their little pollen sacs. It would make the lovely dark apple blossom honey. Then came the summer clover which makes honey as pale and yellow as an oat-field, and then the heavy-scented lime-tree flowers which give honey of palest green. All summer long the bees were at work until, in August, Zachary took the heaviest honey harvest he had ever known.

Always, after that, he kept a fresh bough of juniper hanging in his bee bole, and his honey was always the best in Peckington Parva. Even old Mrs Dunwiddie had to get over her crossness and became his best customer again.

Birch, Ash and Elder

One winter there was much illness in Peckington Parva, and Maisie's parents both died of it. She was a strange silent girl, with hair and eyes as dark as blackberries and skin as pale as cream. Everyone was sorry for her, left, as she was, all alone. The forester and his wife offered her a home in their cottage.

'She'll be company for me, Simon,' said Alice. 'We've no child of our own and we can make her happy.'

So Maisie came to live with them. She was quiet and obedient and did her share of the work around the house. So it was odd that so many things went wrong almost as soon as she came. Milk boiled over, washing fell off the line into the mud, things were lost or tools broken just when they were needed. Alice had headaches and grew thin and pale, and even the cat seemed nervous and would sometimes bite and scratch.

'It's queer,' said Simon. 'There's been ill luck on the house ever since Maisie came.'

Alice wouldn't listen to him.

'Nonsense,' she told him. 'What could Maisie have to do with it? You're hard on the girl, Simon, the poor motherless young thing.'

Simon said no more, but all the same he began to watch his adopted daughter.

One day, after sweeping the kitchen, Maisie looked at the old besom broom.

'It's nearly worn out,' she told Alice. 'I'll go into the wood this afternoon and gather the twigs for a new one.'

She did as she promised, and Simon watched her that evening as she made the broom. She had found a straight thin branch for the handle, and plenty of good strong twigs, with thin whippety young shoots to bind them all together. But after everyone had gone to bed, Simon waited until all was quiet and then crept down to the kitchen and looked carefully at the new broom.

Besoms are nearly always made of birch, but this was different. Birch twigs had indeed been used for the brush itself. But the handle was of ash wood, which protects witches from drowning, and the twigs were bound together by shoots of willow – most sinister of all trees. People said that on a dark night a willow would uproot itself and follow muttering behind a solitary traveller. Simon's heart turned cold as he looked, for birch, ash, and willow together make up a witch's broom.

Tomorrow would be May Day Eve, the last night of April, that the witches call Walpurgis Night. All the witches for miles around would mount their broomsticks and fly to a great meeting on top of the highest hill. He was sure that Maisie meant to join them. He was very afraid, for he knew now that Maisie's quiet ways were trickery, while in her secret heart she really hated her foster-parents.

At last he hit on a plan. Next night he lingered in the kitchen until Alice and Maisie had gone upstairs. Then he took the new broom and quickly broke it in pieces. He threw it on the rubbish heap, fetched in the old broom, and put it back in its place in the corner. Then he went upstairs to bed and listened.

When Alice was fast asleep and the distant church clock struck midnight, he heard Maisie creeping softly down the stairs. He waited for the faint click of the back door before he followed her. He paused in the kitchen to pick up his big forester's axe, then slipped out into the garden.

The moon was full that night. It filled every open space with light and cast long shadows from every bush and tree. Maisie was in the middle of the garden, striding the besom that she held with both hands. Close to her crouched the cat, its back arched and its fur all on end, yowling as it watched. Her eyes glittering in the moonlight, Maisie cried the command that every witch broom must obey.

'Horse and hattock! Away! Away!'

The broom gave a little hop and then stood still. Maisie struck it angrily.

'Hear me! Hear me! Horse and hattock, away! Away!'

Simon stepped out from the shadow.

'That broom will never fly, Maisie. It's a good honest besom, made only of birch. Your new broom is broken.'

Maisie whirled round, her face as pale as the moon and her eyes blazing with anger.

'How dare you? How dare you? I will punish you for this.'

Simon was afraid but still he felt sorry for her.

'Give up this wicked magic,' he begged her. 'It will only make you wretched. Be our true child, our daughter.'

'Your daughter?' sneered the witch. 'What do I want with father or mother? It is I who brought the winter sickness to Peckington Parva, and I who have made your wife ill. I hate you both.'

Anger swept away Simon's pity. He sprang forward to seize her, but she slipped out of his reach.

'Catch me if you can!' she screamed.

Suddenly she was gone, melted away into the moonlight. Simon stared about him, bewildered. The fallen broomstick lay on the grass. He was all alone in the garden. Then a dark shape close to the hedge caught his eye. Moonlight makes all things seem strange. But Simon was sure there had been no bush there before. He looked at it carefully.

It was an elder tree. A witch tree.

For a moment he paused, unwilling to strike. Then he remembered his wife's pale face and tired worried eyes. He raised his axe and struck the tree with all his strength. He thought he heard a faint cry, but still he struck and struck again. As the trunk broke and fell he dragged it across the field to the stream that flowed there deeply. He thrust the branches down into the water until every twig and leaf was covered. Then when the stream ran quiet and smooth again he went back into his house.

The first thing he saw was his wife waiting for him in the kitchen, holding the purring cat in her arms. Her face was rosy and her eyes bright.

'Oh Simon!' she said. 'I feel suddenly so well again, and the house feels happy – as if some dreadful thing had gone away.'

'The dreadful thing *has* gone,' said Simon. 'It will never come back.'

He was right. No one ever saw Maisie, the witch, again, and Simon and Alice lived happily and in peace for the rest of their lives. But if ever a tiny shoot of elder sprung up in his garden – for elders will plant themselves anywhere as every gardener knows – Simon plucked it out and threw it on his bonfire.

Night Riders

The Little People may do good or they may do harm. That is why folk often call them the Good People – as you say 'Good dog' to one that makes you nervous. But Kate heeded no warnings about them. She wanted to see them and see them she would.

On Midsummer Eve, when the fairies ride at midnight, she slipped away from the house when her mother thought she was safely in bed. Quiet as a shadow she crept to the end of the little valley where they were said to ride and hid herself behind a hawthorn bush (and that in itself was foolish enough, for hawthorns are sacred to fairies).

'I'll only look,' she said to herself. 'There can't be any harm in that. I must stay very still, and they'll never see me.'

The stars pricked out and the moon rose. At last, faint but clear, Kate heard the clink of harness, the sweet silver chime of tiny bells, and the clear note of a horn. Suddenly they were there, a troop of the Little People riding up the valley. They were mounted on horses no bigger than hares, yet they looked very kingly. They were dressed in hunting green, and the grey moonlight glinted on their sharp bright eyes, the silver hunting horns, and the little bells that chimed and shone along their bridles. Some had faces as cool and smooth as flowers, others were withered as autumn leaves.

So strange they were that Kate gave a little gasp of surprise.

Instantly the first rider drew rein and all her followers halted. She was taller by an acorn's length than any of the others. Her face was brown and narrow and older than the oldest oak, but she bore herself like a queen. Her voice rang shrill and fierce, and her anger filled the night like a cold wind.

'Come out and be seen, whoever you are. Man or maid, child or babe, mortal eyes have seen what none should see.'

Trembling and afraid Kate crept from her hiding-place. The Little People crowded round her, chattering like angry squirrels. The horses snorted and stamped.

'Please,' begged poor Kate, 'don't be angry. I meant no harm. I only wanted so much to see you. I promise I will never tell.'

'You will never tell,' said the queen harshly, 'for you will never speak again.'

She was raising her hand, spell-wise, when a young man thrust his horse between her and Kate. He was more richly dressed than all the others, and as young and handsome as the queen was old and withered.

'She is but a child, mother,' he said. 'And surely in truth she meant no harm. Let her come with us and all will be well.'

The queen's face softened as she looked at her son. 'I have never refused you anything,' she said. 'Let the girl come with us then, but you yourself must guard her.'

'Trust me,' said the prince, and he held out his hand to Kate. 'Ride with me, mortal child, and see what you will.'

Kate took his hand and was astonished to find herself no bigger than her protector. He lifted her up and set her before him on his horse. The whole troop turned again and rode on up the valley. The way grew narrower and steeper, and the stream below it danced ever more noisily over its stony bed. At last the path ended at the foot of a cliff that barred their way. A fern-fringed waterfall tumbled down it from above. Straight through the rushing water rode the queen and struck her riding whip against the rock.

'Open, rock, and let us in.'

At once the solid rock split and opened, forming a wide portal. Kate felt the cold rush of water as the whole company streamed in, but not even a hair of her head was wet. They rode in a strange still light through an open glade in a forest. The leaves of the trees were silver and gold, and birds as bright as jewels flashed between them. Their songs were so sweet that she could have listened to them for ever. At last they came to a palace with walls that

shimmered like raindrops in the sun. Here they dismounted.

There followed a day of wonders beyond Kate's dreams. The young man never left her side, whether they feasted or danced or wandered through gardens as lovely as Paradise. She wished she could be always with him. But at last she grew tired. She had been a whole day with the Little People, and now she remembered her mother and her family. They would be worried and searching for her. Full of sorrow at her thoughtlessness, she begged the prince to show her the way home.

The young man frowned.

'Are you not happy here? Stay with me, Kate, and all that you see shall be yours.'

But still she thought of her mother and her baby brother. She thought of the green trees beyond the waterfall and the thrush that sang to her every morning when she woke.

'No, no,' she said. 'I have stayed too long already. They will miss me at home and be anxious.'

The prince's face grew sad as she pleaded with him.

'You may not find what you seek,' he told her.

In spite of his warning she persisted.

'Then,' said he, 'you must drink the herb of sleep, for no mortal may see the way of return from this land.'

Kate shivered as she took from him a golden goblet. But when she thought of her mother's troubled face she knew she must drink.

The Little People know as much about herbs as any wise woman in the mortal world. In the goblet of wine the prince had crumbled the tall spires of yellow agrimony, the wayside flower that gives deep untroubled sleep. Kate felt a great drowsiness enfold her as the fairy garden faded from her sight.

Many hours later she awoke. She was lying behind the hawthorn bush where she had hidden at midnight. Now a pale sun shone through mist and the air was cold. Quickly she stood up and hurried towards home.

She was suddenly afraid. She had stolen away in the green of early spring. Now dry leaves crackled under her feet and frost-furred spider webs clung to the bushes. She reached her own garden gate and stopped, staring. There were no curtains at the windows, no one stood at the open door that sagged on its rusty hinges. A bird flew out of a hole in the roof, and thistles choked the path.

Someone walked along the lane and she ran to him in fear.

'What is it? What has happened? Where have they gone?' she cried.

The man looked at her very oddly.

'No one has lived here for years,' he said. 'The family left long ago. People say they waited for a child who never came back, but left when all hope was gone.'

'But I *have* come back,' cried Kate. 'And I left only yesterday.'

She turned blindly from him towards the village,

looking for someone who would know her. The village was changed. Some of the houses were new, the little saplings she remembered in the churchyard had grown into big trees, and all the faces were those of strangers. She fled from them back to the hawthorn bush and flung herself down to weep.

'Kate, Kate, don't cry,' said a voice above her. 'They should have told you long ago. Mortal time and fairy time are never the same. Come now, drink again.'

The prince knelt beside her and held his golden goblet to her lips. Long, long she slept. She never knew when the Little People, in pity, lifted her gently and carried her away. They laid her on a bed of moss and fern in a secret cave far in the forest. She slept through the cold winter, spring, summer, and autumn. She slept through the years, until spiders wove their shimmering nets across the mouth of the cave, and the robin whispered his little sad lullaby. For all that anyone knows, she is sleeping there still.

The story is still told in Peckington Parva of the child who ran away from the village on Midsummer Eve and was never seen again by mortal eyes.

A Pocketful of Magic

The miller was the richest man in Peckington Parva. Sometimes he gave short measure and sometimes he charged too much. One way and another he made so much money that he felt himself too important even to speak to his poorer neighbours.

One day he decided to give a grand party on New Year's Eve. He invited the squire and the gentlemen farmers and the Lord Mayor from the big town, and all the rich people from miles around, but none of the ordinary folk of the village. He sent for Jimmy Needle, the tailor, and ordered a new coat for the occasion, a coat of the very best red cloth with lots of gold buttons and gold braid. He meant to outshine even the Lord Mayor.

'You can bring the coat for a fitting the day before Christmas Eve,' he said.

The day was very near, but the tailor worked hard and brought the coat to him on time. He found the miller standing at his door, shouting at a thin, anxious-looking man.

'No. I won't let you have more flour until you

can pay. Those who don't work can't eat.'

'But I do work,' protested the man. 'I've been ill, but I can pay you next week. You surely won't let a neighbour's children go hungry at Christmas?'

'I don't know you as a neighbour,' declared the miller with a haughty air. 'I don't remember everyone who comes to the mill.'

'We were boys together,' said the shabby man angrily. 'But you wouldn't remember your own mother if she was poor.'

He went sadly on his way. The miller ignored him and called Jimmy Needle into the house. He was still grumbling as he tried on the new coat. Nothing was right for him. He complained that a sleeve was tight, there was a crease in the lining, and there wasn't enough gold braid.

'Take it away,' he said, 'and put everything right by tomorrow, or I won't pay a penny.'

The tailor walked home over the common, thinking about the miller and his poor neighbour. By the light of the rising moon he could see the gorse and the withered bracken beside the path. In a little sheltered hollow a few fern fronds were still green. Long ago his grandmother had told him about ferns. Fern seed gathered at full moon with the left hand only will make the wearer invisible. His grandmother knew the lore of plants and he trusted her wisdom.

Very carefully, with his left hand only, he picked three small leaflets of fern with their seed spores still clinging to the fronds. He slipped them into a pocket of the miller's jacket and looked at the rising moon with the twinkle of a smile in his eyes.

Christmas Eve broke cold, white, and windy. The tailor delivered the coat. This time the miller was satisfied. He put it on at once in high good humour.

'How do I look?' he asked.

'Fine, fine,' said Jimmy. 'You never looked better.'

Feeling very pleased with himself, the miller followed him outside when he left, hoping to show off to anyone passing by.

Just then the wind blew a great gust that slammed the door shut behind him!

The miller was furious, for the maid was away at market and there was no one else in the house to let him in.

'Wait a minute, tailor,' he shouted. 'You must climb up to a window for me.'

But Jimmy Needle was walking away and didn't seem to hear him. The wind blew more strongly and coldly than ever, and despite his warm new coat the miller began to shiver. Then two boys came along the road, whistling cheerfully.

'Here,' said the miller. 'I'll give a silver coin to the one who will climb on my shoulders and get in through that window.'

The boys stared at each other.

'That's funny,' said one. 'I thought I heard someone talking.'

'So did I,' said the other. 'But there's no one else about except us.'

Off they went together, leaving the miller puzzled

as well as angry. He hurried after them, looking for someone to help him. But again and again the same thing happened. Some people were surprised and some were frightened. As they could see no one, they thought they had only imagined hearing a voice.

At last the miller realised the dreadful truth – he was under some strange enchantment that made him invisible. He was frightened now, and very cold and very hungry, for it was long past his dinner-time.

At first he felt sorry only for himself. Then he noticed that some of the villagers had much thinner coats than his or indeed none at all. A few of them would have a poor meal and a small fire even on Christmas Day. Outside one house he met a ragged shivering boy, so thin that the wind must surely blow right through him. He was the son of the man who had wanted more flour. The miller felt ashamed of himself.

'Here!' he said. 'Take my coat and put it on.'

He slipped off his new jacket and the boy gaped at him.

'Lawks-a-mercy!' he cried. 'Where did you come from? I'll swear you weren't there a second ago.'

'Bless the boy!' shouted the miller joyfully. 'He can see me! Praise be, the spell must be broken. He can really see me. Take my coat, boy, and put it on.'

Wonderingly the boy took the jacket. He felt the good cloth all over, and slid his frozen hand into one of the pockets. Then, hardly daring to believe his luck, he put it on. Neither of them noticed the three small crumpled bits of fern that fell from his fingers and blew away on the wind.

The miller wouldn't stop to listen to the boy's thanks. Almost dancing in his joy he hurried home. The maid had returned and let him in, astonished to see her master in his shirt sleeves on such a bitter day.

'Don't fuss, woman,' said the miller. 'We've other things to think about. After my party on New Year's Eve, there will be another on New Year's Day.'

And so there was. On New Year's Eve he entertained all his rich guests, and wore his second-best coat, and was rather bored by the company. But on New Year's Day everyone in the village was invited – grandparents and parents and children and maiden aunts and solitary uncles and the old man who lived all by himself at the top of the hill – and they sang and danced and made merry until midnight. Never was there such a splendid party. And as long as the miller lived, no one in Peckington Parva ever went hungry again.

The Grateful Mermaid

Peckington Parva is not many miles inland. There is sometimes a salty tang on the rough winter winds, when old traditional tales of the sea are told to the children round the fire. A favourite story is that of the grateful mermaid.

Evan the fisherman was walking across the beach in the cool of the morning. The sun was only just rising. Its light ran smooth and level across the undented sand as the tide ebbed. He thought he was quite alone until he heard the crying.

It came from the tumble of rocks and boulders below the cliff. Evan stopped to listen. At first it had seemed like the mewing of the gulls, but now he heard it more clearly. Out of sight, but not far away, someone was sobbing bitterly.

Evan hurried towards the sound, expecting to find someone fallen and injured among the rocks. But when he saw what it was, his heart began to beat in his ears like a drum.

Lying in a deep rock pool was a girl more beautiful, yet more strange, than he had ever seen. Her hair was green-gold, the colour of unripe wheat, and her eyes glinted like sea sparkles under a midday sun. Her skin was smooth and pale. Below her waist she was the shape of a fish, covered in shining scales of red and gold.

Evan knew well enough what he had found, and he wanted nothing to do with her. This was a mermaid, and he knew many tales of how such creatures had lured men to their deaths in the sea. He would have hurried away but she called to him. Her voice seemed a sighing echo of the waves.

'Evan! Evan! Help me!'

'How do you know me?' he asked roughly, for this made him even more alarmed.

'I saw you out in the bay when you were fishing,' said the mermaid. 'You have a good face and a kind one. Lift me up, Evan, and carry me back to the sea. I fell asleep and the ebb tide has stranded me here.'

'The sea will take you again at the flood,' said Evan – for he was mortally afraid to touch her.

'Cruel, cruel!' cried the mermaid. 'I cannot live till then. See how I wither already in this dry air, and the sun will soon burn me.'

She held out her arms in entreaty. Evan saw that a film of greyness already clouded them.

His heart softened although he was still afraid. Neither woman nor fish, she was still a living creature, and he hated to see anything suffer. He bent towards her.

'You'll not harm me?' he asked.

She smiled at him, sly and secret.

'Why should I harm you, handsome fisherman? Carry me home.'

Her arms clung suddenly about his neck, her tail curled round him. Evan turned and walked swiftly and steadily down to the sea. With every step her grip seemed tighter and her nails dug sharp as a gull's claws into his shoulder. He stopped when the first shallow ripple touched his feet and would have set her down. She clung fiercely to him.

'Further in! Further in! I cannot swim here.'

He carried her beyond the third wave, but still she urged him.

'Further in! Further in!'

Now he was terribly afraid. He thought of the bones of the drowned sailors that mermaids had carried to the bottom of the sea.

'Let me go!' he begged her. 'I have done as you asked. I have saved your life. Will you repay me by taking mine?'

Her strange eyes looked into his, and slowly she loosed her hands.

'No,' she said. 'No. I would have kept you if I could, but not against your will. One day you will be glad that you helped me.'

Sleek and smooth as a fish she slid away, the water rippled and he saw nothing but the sunlit waves and the flying gulls.

Months went by and Evan almost forgot the mermaid. He fell in love with a village girl, and they were to be married at high summer. But the girl became ill, and no one knew how to cure her. Every day she grew weaker and thinner and more faded. One evening, desperate at heart, Evan was walking along the cliff. Below him the surge of a full tide rose and fell with a quiet whisper. Suddenly he heard a splash as if a huge fish had leaped.

'Evan ! Evan !'

Smiling up at him was the mermaid, her green-gold hair floating on the waves.

'Evan ! Foolish Evan !

'Will you let the bonny maid die in your hand,
When the mugwort's in flower all over the land ?'

With a flash of her red-gold scales she leaped again and was gone. Evan gazed round him. All over the waste ground between the cliff and the village grew the tall button-flowered mugwort, its leaves – dark green above and white beneath – flickering in the light wind. He knew what he must do. Quickly he gathered a great bunch of it and carried it home. He boiled it and pounded it and mixed it with wine and honey and gave it to the girl to drink. Soon afterwards the fever left her and day by day she grew stronger. They married at Michaelmas.

Many times after that Evan looked for the mermaid to thank her for her kindness. The tides came and went, but he never saw her again.

The Loving Cup

Lizzie was the silliest girl in Peckington Parva. She cooked everything too much or too little. She muddled the sugar and salt; she let the milk boil over. She hated housework and didn't know one end of a needle from the other. But she was so pretty that half the young men in the village wanted to marry her. Among them were Robert the rich farmer and Peter the poor schoolmaster. Lizzie cared for none of them.

Peter thought of her all day and dreamed of her all night. At last he grew desperate.

'They say there's a white witch lives beyond the hill,' he said to himself one day. 'Perhaps she has a potion that will make Lizzie love me.'

He thought such a potion would cost a great deal. He put together all the money that he had, though it was little enough. He added one or two trinkets that had been his mother's, and set out. It was a long way over the hill, and as he walked he had time to feel frightened. Although a white witch never meddles with black magic, she studies the qualities of plants and the ways of animals, and has much strange and secret knowledge, and powers that seem magical. She would likely be an old, old woman, he thought, and would perhaps be angry at being disturbed.

The white witch lived in a small house set in a sunny garden full of sweet-smelling herbs and the heavy hum of bees. It was too late to change his mind, so Peter thought of pretty Lizzie and marched up the path as boldly as he could. The door opened at once to his knock.

He saw a woman as young as himself, not pretty like Lizzie, but with clear bright eyes and a face as calm as summer. Her hands were rough and brown and scratched – gardener's hands – and she wore a coarse sacking apron. Peter stared at her in surprise.

'I-I-I came to see the white witch,' he stammered. 'Will she let me speak with her?'

The girl laughed. 'That she will,' she said. 'Come in. I am Alison, and some folk do say that I'm a witch.'

He followed her into the cottage. There were pots of flowers everywhere, bunches of herbs hung drying from the ceiling, and ranged on the shelves were jars and pots and bottles of jewelled liquids winking in the sun.

'Tell me your need,' she said, 'and I will help if I can.'

So Peter told her all about pretty careless Lizzie and his love for her. Alison's face grew sad as she listened.

'Will she make you a good wife, Peter? Are you sure you want to marry her.'

'As sure as I'm sitting here,' said Peter. 'I think I shall die if she won't have me.'

Alison sighed and laughed. 'I'd rather you didn't die,' she said. 'I'll give you a love charm. But make sure you stay close by as she drinks, for once she has taken it she'll love the next man she sees beside her.'

She took from a jar the dried and powdered petals of wild cyclamen, that country people call sow-bread because pigs like to eat them. A patch of them, both pink and white, grew in her garden. The upturned rings of petals were like tiny butterflies. She poured on them a ruby-bright liquid, and gave him the mixture in a little phial.

'Mix it with wine,' she told him. 'It will smell so delicious that your Lizzie will long to drink it.'

Joyfully Peter thanked her and poured out on the table his little stock of treasure.

'No,' said Alison, 'I'll not be paid. Love isn't to be bought or sold. Take your charm and go.'

Still Peter insisted, and at last she picked up an old silver locket with a twist of hair inside it.

'Whose is the hair in this?' she asked.

'It was mine, as a child,' said Peter shyly. 'The locket was my mother's.'

'Then this I will keep,' said Alison. 'One gift for another.'

Peter hurried back towards Peckington Parva, anxious to find Lizzie as soon as he could. But even

as he thought of her he thought too of Alison, and his step grew slower and slower.

It was a hot, still, drowsy evening. As he drew near to the village, who should he see but Lizzie herself, fast asleep in the shade of a tree! Peter stood still and looked down at her.

She was indeed very pretty, but he noticed for the first time how her lips pouted. Her hands were small and smooth, not strong and brown and scratched like Alison's. Her skirt was of silk, uncreased and fresh, too fine for working in. *She* would never wear a sacking apron.

'Pretty Lizzie,' he said softly. 'I hope you will be happy.'

Just then he heard the sound of hooves, and looked up to see farmer Robert riding back from his harvest field. From the young man's saddle hung a straw basket still holding his unfinished bread and cheese and half a flagon of wine. Peter went to meet him.

'Good evening to you, Farmer Robert,' he said. 'And good fortune too, for surely your fortune lies there. Pour this into your wine and offer it to Lizzie when she wakes. I promise she'll look on you kindly.'

Robert took the little phial but stared at Peter in amazement.

'A love charm? Is that what you offer me? But I thought you wanted Lizzie for yourself!'

'So I did,' admitted Peter. 'But you are rich enough to keep a wife like Lizzie, and I'm too poor ever to make her happy.'

There and then he turned and walked back the way he had come, up the hill and over and down the other side. The moon was already up when he reached the white witch's cottage, but she saw him standing at her gate in the twilight and came out to meet him.

'Did the charm not work?' she asked him.

'I hope it worked well,' said Peter, 'but not for me. Love charms are for those who don't know their own minds. But I want a girl who is wise and good, who will love me of her own free will.'

The white witch laughed and put her hands in his.

Peter never went back to Peckington Parva. He and Alison married, and he learned the art of herbs – those that give sleep, those that heal wounds, those that take away warts, and many other things. People from far and near brought their troubles to them, and no one ever went away without help.

As for Robert and Lizzie, they too were very happy. Robert was proud of his pretty and loving wife, and Lizzie delighted in having as many dresses as there are weeks in the year.

The Mountains of the Moon

If ever there was a cross-grained, sour-faced, selfish old man, it was Andrew Sillikin. He struck a hard bargain and would always keep to it, but he cared not a penny for anyone. One hot day as he worked in his garden a stranger stopped at his gate – a tall, thin, scarecrow of a man, with bold dark eyes and a crooked smile. Andrew didn't fancy his looks at all.

'On your way,' he said sharply. 'We want no beggars round here.'

'Who said I was a beggar?' demanded the stranger. 'I've asked nothing of you, have I? Though, since you've been civil enough to speak to me,' – his smile broadened – 'I could do with a drink of cold water on a day like this.'

Andrew straightened up, put a hand to his back, and groaned.

'Do you think *I* can draw from the well for you – a poor, stiff, old man like me?'

'Is the pain that bad?' said the tall man. 'Then you shouldn't be working this big garden without help. I'll finish weeding that row for you if you'll give me a mug of cider in return.'

Nimble as a cat, he jumped the gate and took hold of the fork before Andrew could stop him. The old man was really rather tired and glad of a rest, though he wouldn't admit it. So, grumbling a bit, he fetched a mug of cider, taking care not to fill it to the brim. When he came back with it the job was already finished.

'You work fast,' he admitted grudgingly.

The stranger nodded.

'I'm a good gardener, Master. You'll not find a better. I need work and you need help. Let's strike a bargain. Will you take me on?'

'I won't,' said old Andrew. 'What, give a job to any gypsy fellow who stops at the gate? You've had your cider, now be off with you!'

'I'm no gypsy,' said the man. 'But like the gypsies I know much about herbs and plants. Employ me, and no man in Peckington Parva will be more proud of his garden.'

'No,' said Andrew.

But the fellow went on persuading, with a mischievous glint in his eye, and Andrew went on refusing until at last he lost his temper.

'I'll employ you when rabbits grow wings,' he shouted. 'I'll employ you when I can fly to the mountains of the moon!'

The stranger's crooked smile flashed out.

'It's a bargain,' he declared.

'A bargain, what do you mean?' blustered Andrew.

'That you'll employ me when you can fly to the mountains of the moon. You've just said so.'

'You must be mad,' said Andrew. 'That was only a manner of speaking.'

'But you said it,' answered the stranger softly. 'And I don't like folk who break a promise. Come now, when you can fly to the mountains of the moon you'll make me your gardener?'

Andrew stared. The fellow must certainly be mad. If he humoured him, perhaps he would go away.

'Very well,' he agreed, 'if that satisfies you. But it can never happen.'

The stranger struck the old man's palm with a hand as hard and brown as bark.

'Done!' he declared. 'We'll have a drink to seal the bargain.'

'Have it and welcome, if you'll go and leave me alone,' grumbled Andrew.

The tall man followed him as he went into the kitchen, but paused a moment beside the flower-bed near the door. Among the poppies and larkspur and snapdragons was a patch of blue – the drooping heads of aconite that is sometimes called monkshood or wolf-bane. He snapped off two or three as he passed.

The old man drew two mugs of cider and set them on the table, then turned to tighten the tap on the barrel. He never saw the stranger's strong brown fingers hover above his drink, squeezing the juice of the blue petals into it.

'Good health, my friend!' said the stranger gravely.

He lifted his mug and so did Andrew – prepared to be pleasant if only it would make his visitor go away. They drank to the last drop.

'That's queer,' said Andrew. 'I feel as if-as if- '

He sat down abruptly. He seemed to be falling asleep although his eyes stayed open. The tall man smiled to himself and laid his hand on the old man's head, murmuring strange words:

'Wolf-bane
Still your brain.
Monkshood
Still your blood.
Aconite,
Fly-by-night,
Fill your mind with dreams of flight.'

'Flying . . . flying . . . flying . . .' muttered Andrew.

'Yes, you are flying,' said the stranger softly. 'How high you are! Over the roof-top. Over the church spire. Over the clouds. Up among the stars. See how the stars stream past you!'

Andrew laughed in his strange sleep, and reached out his hands as if to catch the stars.

'And now! Now!' whispered the stranger. 'What's that beneath you? The cold, cold light, the shadows deep as midnight, and the sharp white peaks?'

'Mountains! Mountains!' muttered Andrew. 'The mountains of the moon!'

The man laughed aloud. He dipped a cup in the bucket of spring water that stood by the door and

shook the drops of it over the old man's face. Andrew stirred and shook himself and ran his hands through his hair.

'Bless me!' he said. 'That was the oddest thing! I thought I was flying, flying.'

'So you were,' said the stranger. 'I saw you go and I saw you come. Right over the mountains of the moon you've been, with the midnight shadows and their sharp white peaks.'

''Twas so indeed,' agreed the old man. 'And a wonderful thing it were. Darn me if I know how it happened, but it did. And I've never broken a bargain.'

So the stranger stayed and looked after old Andrew's garden. The old man never had cause to regret it. Sometimes he remembered his strange journey with wonder and pleasure – but he never knew that he had drunk aconite, the juice that witches smear on their broomsticks before they mount them to fly to their midnight meetings. The stranger certainly knew about plants and herbs and how to use them safely – which was just as well since some of them are deadly.

Blackdown Market

If you live in Somerset you will already know, like the children of Peckington Parva, that the fairies hold a market on Blackdown Hill every Midsummer Eve. If you have good sense and good manners you won't go near it, for the Little People don't like to be seen.

Unluckily for him, Farmer Bodger had little sense and no manners. On Midsummer Eve he'd been to Taunton sheep fair, and he'd had too much good Somerset cider before he set off for home again. It made him bold and stupid.

'Reckon I'll go over Blackdown,' he said to himself, 'and see if it's true about that there fairy market that folks tell on.'

It was already pitch black when he reached Blackdown, and at first he could see and hear nothing. Then he pulled up his horse and listened. Further up the hill and not far ahead was a rustle and a stir although there was no breath of wind. He urged his horse forward. Now he could hear whispering sounds and thin cries like bird-calls.

'That's it!' he exclaimed. 'That's it for certain sure. Danged if I don't go and see 'un for myself.'

The horse sweated with fright, and shivered and laid back its ears as if to warn him of danger. But Bodger wouldn't heed him. He struck him and kicked him on, never caring what his big hooves might trample down.

Still he could see nothing. But suddenly out of the dark came a small uproar of sounds, as if little tables were turned over, crockery broken, money bags spilled open, and above it all the angry babble of shrill bat-like voices.

He felt hands clawing at his legs, small and hard and sharp, as if a whole flock of starlings were tearing and beating at him. Unseen creatures swarmed up him, knocked off his hat, scratched his face, and tugged at the horse's mane and tail until the poor terrified creature reared and threw him.

Bodger fell so hard that he lost his senses. When he recovered it was daylight and he was all alone on the cold wet grass of Blackdown Hill. His horse had gone, galloping home sweating and covered with foam. Bodger had to walk all the way – and very hard it was, for he was sore and stiff and aching all over, and his right leg was lame for many weeks afterwards.

His neighbour, Farmer Hackett, was sorry for Bodger when he heard about it.

'But what can you expect,' he said, 'if you disturb the Little People so rudely?'

All the same, he helped Bodger with his hay-making and his sheep-dipping, for he was a kind-hearted man. He was as unlike his neighbour as he could be, hard-working and cheerful, with a good word for everyone. Every night he was careful to leave a clean and tidy hearth in his kitchen, with a pail of fresh spring water and a dish of cream beside it, ready for the fairies.

Next Midsummer Eve it happened that Farmer Hackett had ridden over to Taunton, and his way home lay over Blackdown Hill. He hurried to cross it in daylight so that he shouldn't disturb the Little People. The day was very hot and his horse was so tired that he dismounted to let the beast graze and rest for a while. He gathered a great handful of grass and clover and pushed it under the horse's headband to protect his head and ears from the sun. Another handful, cool and fragrant, he put inside his own hat for the same purpose.

He never knew that among the grass he had picked a four-leaved clover!

He lay down in the shade of a furze while his horse was grazing. But the sun was so warm and the bees hummed so drowsily that he soon fell asleep.

It was nearly dark when he woke. Up he jumped in a terrible hurry, mounted and pressed on as fast as he could.

'Eh,' he said to himself. 'Careless old fool that I be to waste so much time! I wouldn't for the world disturb them little dears.'

He rode as quietly as he could, stopping now and then to listen. Night was falling quickly and in his haste he mistook his path. He reined in his horse, afraid to move further. The branch of a tree touched his face and he put up a hand to brush it away.

He felt the curved zig-zag shape of the leaves, and that made him more anxious than ever. For he had halted beneath an oak tree, and he knew the ancient rhyme:

Fairy folk
Do live in oak.

And at that moment he saw lights, hundreds of tiny lights, like powdered stars all over the grass ahead of him.

'That's it!' he said. 'That's it! It must be the fairy market. But how come I can see the lights of it?'

He scratched his head in bewilderment, and as he did so he felt the wad of grass and clover still inside his hat.

'Dang me!' said Farmer Hackett. 'If that don't beat all! There must be a four-leaved clover among the rest – the leaf that gives sight of the fairies. The good luck leaf too. I'll take the risk whatever it costs me.'

Very quietly he slipped off his horse and crept forward.

'I won't disturb 'un,' he said. 'Whatever happens, 'twould be worth it just to see the little dears.'

Next moment he stood quite still, staring, his mouth wide open in excitement and surprise. Hundreds of small people bustled to and fro almost at his feet. They wore jackets of scarlet and jackets of blue, and circlets of gold were set in their thistle-down hair. They were talking and bargaining, buy-

ing and selling, at little stalls set out just like those in the big market at Taunton. The counters were loaded with fruit and vegetables and flowers and pots and pans and pretty knick-knacks, as gay and colourful as you please.

Farmer Hackett was so delighted by them that he forgot to be cautious. He moved forward, stepping very carefully so as not to hurt anything with his big feet.

When the fairies saw him walking so gently and looking so happy, they greeted him politely with every sign of welcome.

'It's Farmer Hackett,' said one. 'Him that puts out the spring water and the cream for us every night.'

'Good evening to you, Farmer Hackett,' said another. 'What will you buy?'

There was a tiny cider mug on his stall, no bigger than the farmer's thumb, but the prettiest he'd ever seen.

'I'd dearly like that little mug there,' said Hackett.

He took a gold coin out of his pocket and laid it gently on the stall. The fairy looked at it and gave him a little pile of dead oak leaves for change, as serious as could be. He wrapped the mug in a big dock leaf. Hackett put it in his pocket and – not to hurt the fairy's feelings – picked up the leaves for change just as if they were real money. Then he bade them all goodnight and went back to his horse, still stepping very carefully, and rode home as if in a dream.

When he reached his own kitchen he put the little cider mug on the table and the oak leaves all round it.

'Fairy things!' he said. 'They'll all have vanished in the morning. But 'twere worth it just to see the little dears.'

And he went to bed.

Sure enough, when he came downstairs next morning the fairy cup and the oak leaves had gone. In their place was a splendid silver cider mug with pieces of gold all round it. Farmer Hackett drank from it every night all his life after. And from that day onwards, his was the luckiest farm in all Somerset.

Visitors

A woodman and his wife lived in a small house deep in the forest where he worked. They had a little girl whom they loved very much, but they also wanted a son.

At last a baby was born to them, as fine a boy as anyone ever had. He was to be christened at home, for it was too far for his mother to carry him to the church in Peckington Parva. The time before christening is dangerous, because the fairies will sometimes snatch an unbaptised child – especially if it is beautiful – and leave a sickly one of their own in its place.

One evening the woodman came home from work to find his little daughter playing with another child. His wife was out of sight, picking fruit in the garden.

'Who is this?' asked the woodman.

'She came out of the trees to play with me,' said the little girl.

The woodman's heart turned cold. The child had slipped past him into the house before he could stop her, but in three strides he stood between it and

the cradle where his son lay sleeping. The child looked at him sidelong.

'I only want a drink of water,' she said. 'I'm thirsty.'

'Very well,' said the woodman.

But he didn't go out into the kitchen. He stayed, and always watching her, dipped a cup in a bowl of water that stood near the cradle. It wasn't the water from the well that they used every day. It had been drawn sparkling and pure from St Katherine's Spring on the hill and carried down ready for the christening.

'Blessed be the water,' said the woodman, and gave her the cup.

She looked up at him with her child's face, but her eyes were as old as the forest itself. As the water touched her lips she screamed and threw down the cup.

'Bitter, bitter!' she cried, and fled back into the forest.

The woodman called his wife to stay with the baby, while he walked to a nearby thicket. He cut a great bough of spindle, brought it home, and hung it on the house door. The pink seed cases had split open to show the glowing orange berries inside.

'That will keep the infant safe,' he said, 'for fairy folk can't abide spindle. They're afeared of it.'

Next day his daughter was playing outside when a child came softly out of the wood. She was so laughing and lively that the little one wanted her to stay.

'Then first throw away those berries on the door,'

coaxed the child, 'for I don't like them.'

The woodman's little girl stretched up and pulled down the bough of spindle – and in that very instant the child slipped through into the house. But the father was there and he stepped quickly in front of the cradle.

'What do you want?' he asked sternly.

'Only a bite to eat,' whined the child. 'I'm hungry.'

The woodman laid his hands on the crusty loaf that stood on the table.

'Blessed be bread,' he said, 'that gives us life.'

He broke off a piece and gave it to her. She looked at him sly and sideways with a child's eyes, but took the bread in a hand as pale and withered and freckled as a dead sycamore leaf. But as it touched her lips she hurled it away.

'Burning, burning!' she cried, and fled back into the forest.

This time the woodman went further up the hill until he found a rowan tree, its berries all ablaze in the sunshine. He cut a great bough of it and hung it on the house door.

'That will keep us safe,' he said, 'for the fairy folk are even more afeared of rowan than of spindle.'

He told his little daughter that she was not to touch the berries. But next day, as she wandered out to play, a child came again from the wood to join her. She danced and sang and played and teased until her companion forgot all about her father's warning.

'Pull down that branch from the door so that we can play with it,' said the child.

And the instant the rowan was tugged away she opened the door and ran in.

The woodman stood with outstretched arms in front of the cradle.

'What do you want?' he demanded.

'A gift,' begged the child. 'A gift as small as you like, for I'm that poor, anything will do.'

'You shall have a gift,' said the woodman.

He took from his work-bench two iron nails – iron that has been sacred since the beginning of time – and bound them with a piece of string to form a cross.

The creature watched him with its child's face, but its hair was whiter than December frost. It shrunk away trembling as he held up the nails, then fled shrieking from the house.

'Lost, lost, lost!' it squalled, and its voice died away into the forest faint and shrill as the cry of a lapwing over an empty marsh.

The woodman's son was christened that very same day, and the fairy folk never troubled the house again.

Glossary

ACONITE (or MONKS HOOD): A tall slender plant bearing hood-shaped purple flowers in May. It grows best in damp shady places.

AGRIMONY: A plant with tall stiff hairy stems, ending in spikes of small yellow flowers from July to August. Found on roadsides and waste places, especially on chalky soil.

APPLE: Apple trees with their smooth grey bark are smothered in pink blossom in April. Most apples ripen in September or October.

ASH: One of our largest trees, with rough ridged grey bark. Its leaves are made up of narrow leaflets. In spring it is the only tree with stiff grey twigs ending in short fat black buds.

BIRCH: A tall slender tree with a silvery white trunk, and small pointed leaves that dance even in the lightest wind. It grows wild in woodland clearings and also in many gardens.

BRACKEN: One of the tallest ferns, with jagged fronds that are pale green in spring, turn very dark in late summer, and rusty brown in autumn. It grows everywhere on uncultivated sandy soil.

CLOVER: A creeping plant with sweetly-scented globe-shaped heads of pink or greenish white flowers all through the summer. The small leaves are usually divided into three leaflets, but very rarely you may find a lucky one with four.

CYCLAMEN: The frail pink or white flowers, each a ring of upturned petals, are very rare in the wild, but are often seen in gardens in late summer and autumn. The big round dark-green leaves have pale marbled markings.

ELDER: A very common shrub in woods and hedgerows, bearing heavily scented clusters of white flowers in June and July, followed by bunches of black berries.

HAWTHORN (or MAY): This grows either as a tree or a hedgerow. In May it is covered with white honey-scented blossom. In spring the small irregular leaves are a very vivid green. Country people sometimes call it 'bread and cheese'.

HAZEL: A small tree from which we get cobnuts. In spring it carries long yellow catkins, and also tiny scarlet ones that look like buds. It grows everywhere in woods and hedgerows.

HERB-TWOPENCE: A little spreading plant with small round leaves. It bears tiny open yellow flowers all summer long, and grows mostly in damp places.

HOLLYHOCK: A very tall garden plant. The big leaves are heart-shaped and rough. Frilly, open flowers, red, pink, yellow, or white, grow in bunches close to the stalks all through the summer.

JUNIPER: An evergreen tree that grows from a rounded base to a point at the top. The dark-green narrow leaves are prickly to touch, and have a sharp clean scent. It is mostly grown in gardens.

LAUREL: A shrub with big thick oval leaves, dark green and sometimes spotted with yellow. It is grown everywhere in gardens and parks.

MARIGOLD: The wild plant has flat golden flowers all summer. The stalks are tough and wiry, with narrow leaves that grow in pairs up the stem. It grows anywhere on waste ground.

MUGWORT: A plant with tall stout ribbed stems, reddish in colour. The toothed green leaves are white and woolly underneath. From July to September it bears long narrow clusters of pale button-shaped flowers. It grows at the roadside and on waste-land.

ROWAN (or Mountain Ash): A tall slender tree with leaves made up of many light-green leaflets. In May and June it bears clusters of small white flowers, followed in autumn by brilliant scarlet berries. It likes open ground and hilly country.

SPINDLE: A small shrub with grey bark and oval, pointed leaves. It bears small greenish flowers in June and July, followed in autumn by bright pink lobe-shaped fruits that split open to show the orange-coloured seeds inside. It is found anywhere in copses or hedges.

WILD THYME: A herb which has little circles of tiny purple flowers all up its stems from June to August. Its scent is like that of the cultivated herb. It grows mostly on dry open ground.

WILLOW: A tree with slender drooping branches. The leaves, like long fingers, are pale green above and silver-white beneath, so that they shimmer in the wind. They love water and often grow on the banks of rivers or streams.

The village of
PECKINGTON
PARVA
Blackdown hill
Miller's house
Kate's house
← To the waterfall
Giles' cottage
Zachary's cottage
Jack's farm